The Protector Bug

The Tryouts

SATURDAY ONLY!

Annual Protector Bug try outs

Only **3** will be chosen

by
JASON REID

Thank you to my wife, Kim, and my children, Derek, Ashlyn, Kyle and Ryan for putting up with all my crazy ideas.

I would also like to thank Beldean Ciprian, who managed the illustration process as well as Alexandra Abagiu, the talented artist who made this book come alive. They are both from Deveo Media Studio (www.deveomedia.com) – Check them out!

Sheldon, a mild mannered ant, and his best friend Jared, a muscular mosquito, rushed towards the tunnel entrance.

"Hurry buddy, we're going to be late! I don't want to miss this," Jared said excitedly.

Out of breath, Sheldon replied, "You know, I'm not a runner. I'm going as fast as I can!"

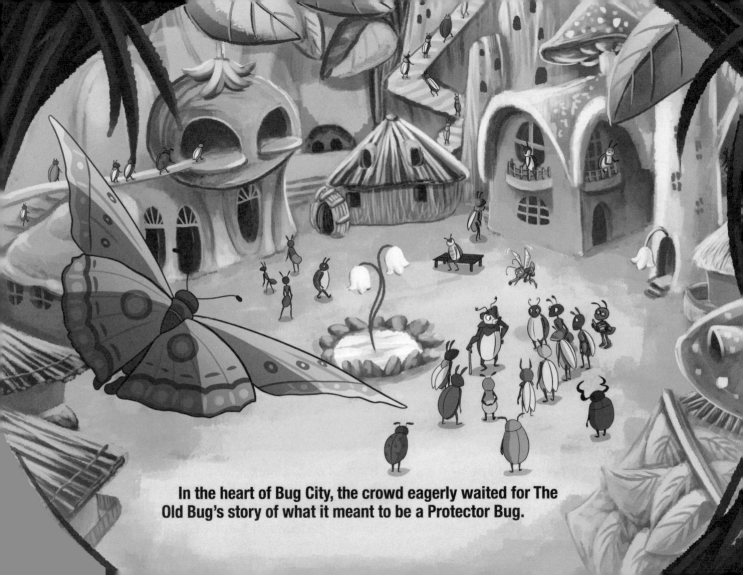

In the heart of Bug City, the crowd eagerly waited for The Old Bug's story of what it meant to be a Protector Bug.

"The closest call I ever had was back in '62," The Old Bug recalled. "I was on patrol with my best friend, Perry. We were at a little girl's house. I think her name was Alice. We'd just landed on her bedside table when I looked down and there they were: tentacles, slithering out from under the bed. They smelled horrible, like Brussels sprouts and rotting cheese, but I jumped into action and drove my sword into the slimy creature."

"These creatures travel in pairs," he said. "Perry was busy fighting one that was coming out of the closet when all of a sudden I found myself wrapped in those stinking tentacles about to have the green squeezed out of me!"

"Perry came to my rescue, as he often did. We fought those slimy monsters through the entire night. My best friend and I were determined to protect Alice from those disgusting-smelling tentacles. Alice quietly slept unharmed, totally unaware that we were even there. That is what Protector Bugs do."

"We kept fighting that creature all night. Finally, the sun came up, Alice arose and all was calm. Perry and I were exhausted, but we had won! Another child was kept safe and sound as she slept."

The Old Bug stood on a stump with his cane held high in the air. The young bugs cheered.

"Tomorrow's the big day!" Jared announced to Sheldon. "The Protector Bug Tryouts. We will be just like The Old Bug and his buddy, Perry, fighting side by side to make sure kids can sleep through the night."

"I'm not doing it," Sheldon sheepishly answered.

"I mean, I want to, but I can't. I'm not cut out for fighting and stuff. I'm meant for other stuff, just like my dad says."

"But...but...we've been planning this since we were baby larva. We have to be Protector Bugs together!" a visibly frustrated Jared said.

"You two will never be Protector Bugs! There are only three spots and they belong to us!"

The Beetle brothers, Buster, Biff and Buzz, stood tall and mean, arms crossed, glaring down the path at Jared and Sheldon.

"Let's make this perfectly clear," Buster threatened as he and Biff pushed Sheldon to the ground. "You ain't gonna be in that race. You ain't a Protector Bug! Heck, you can't even stand on your own legs!"

"Keep that nose out of my face, mosquito!" Buzz yelled. "Pa says the only real Protector Bugs are Beetles, and we're going to be the next three!"

"Not if I have a say!" a defiant Jared screamed back.

By dinnertime, Sheldon had forgotten all about the Beetles. While dinner was being served, he and his dad (like father, like son) were happily reading away. Sheldon's mother looked at the two, took a deep breath and asked Sheldon, "So dear, are you going to try out for the Protector Bugs tomorrow?"

Sheldon's dad looked surprised. "There are plenty of important jobs besides being a Protector Bug," he said, "like gathering food or watching out for hungry birds like I do. I mean, if everyone was a Protector Bug, who would sound the warning bell when birds fly into town?"

"Dad, did you ever want to be a Protector Bug?" Sheldon asked.

"Son, bugs like you and me are meant to use our minds, not our muscles," he answered.

"Poppycock!" exclaimed Sheldon's mom. "You can be whatever you want to be Sheldon! I think you would make the best Protector Bug ever!"

Sheldon sadly stared at his plate. "That's OK, Mom. Dad's right. There are better jobs for bugs   like me." Sheldon's dad smiled. "That's the sensible thing son."

Sheldon sat in his bedroom, trying to get his mind off the dinner conversation. A firefly buzzed around his head as a box of Protector Bug comics spilled out all over his mattress. He turned to his firefly friend and pleadingly said, "I really wish I could be one, you know."

"What if your dad is wrong?" his friend asked. "What if being a Protector Bug is not about how big your muscles are? Why can't they choose a Protector Bug based on how smart you are or how good of a person you are? Why does it have to be a race?"

Sheldon's mom peaked into her husband's office.

"I see you dug up the old flyer. You would have made an amazing Protector Bug, dear."

A little startled, he looked up and replied, "Not for me, dear. I had other things to do...important things...plus, I had you and Sheldon to take are of. That is all the protecting I needed to do."

Buster - 9
Buzz - 8,8
Jared - 8
Biff - 7

On competition day, everyone in Bug City came out to see the games. The scoreboard showed the standings. Two of the Beetle brothers, Buster and Buzz, were in first and second place. Jared was in third, followed by Biff Beetle. The scores were very close.

Buster – 9

Buzz – 8,5

Jared – 8

Biff – 7

The final contest was a foot race. The bugs lined up on the starting line.

"Back of the line, mosquito," said Buster.

"Yea, that's where you belong!" said Biff.

"We'll see about that," Jared told them.

The race wound its way down to the stream. Jared was in the lead. As he continued to sprint in front of the pack, he heard someone yelling in the distance.

"Help! Help! I'm stuck," shouted a stranded bug.

The little bug was on a sinking makeshift raft, trapped by a fallen log.

Knowing he was about to lose the race and his chance at being the next Protector Bug, Jared slowed, "Ah shoot!" He turned back to the unfortunate bug and yelled, "Hold on, I'll save you."

"Oh, thank you! I can't move this log by myself and I'm afraid I might drown," the bug said gratefully. "Don't worry, we'll move it together."

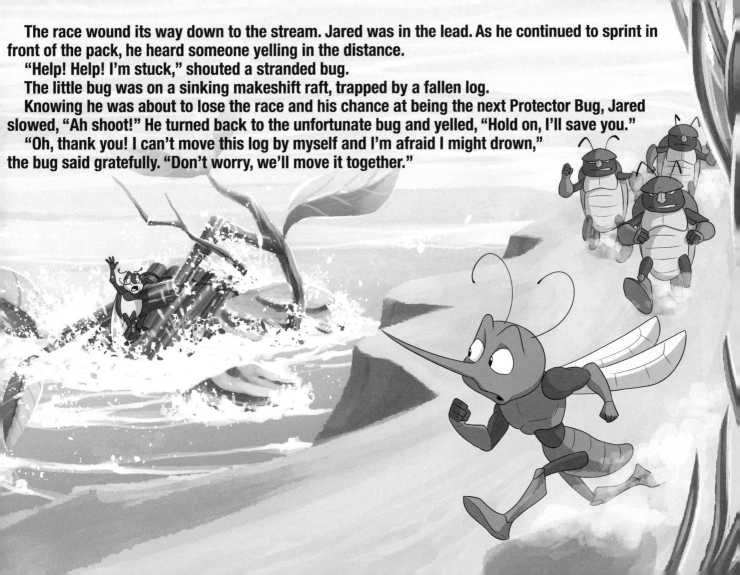

The Beetle brothers slowed down just enough to watch Jared leave for the stranded bug.
"Guys, come give me a hand with this log, this little guy is stuck," Jared pleaded to them.
"You've got it. You're strong, aren't you?" yelled Buster.
"Yeah, you don't need us," said Biff.
"We'll come back and check on you after the race," said Buzz.
"After we get our trophies of course," laughed Buster.
And off they went.

Jared and the stranded bug used all their strength to move the log. They were slowly making progress, but it looked like the worst was over.

"Are you in a race?" asked the stranded bug.

"Yeah, kind of, I guess," Jared replied.

"And you stopped to help me?" asked the bug gratefully.

"Let's get you to safety. There'll be other races, um, I hope," a dejected Jared said.

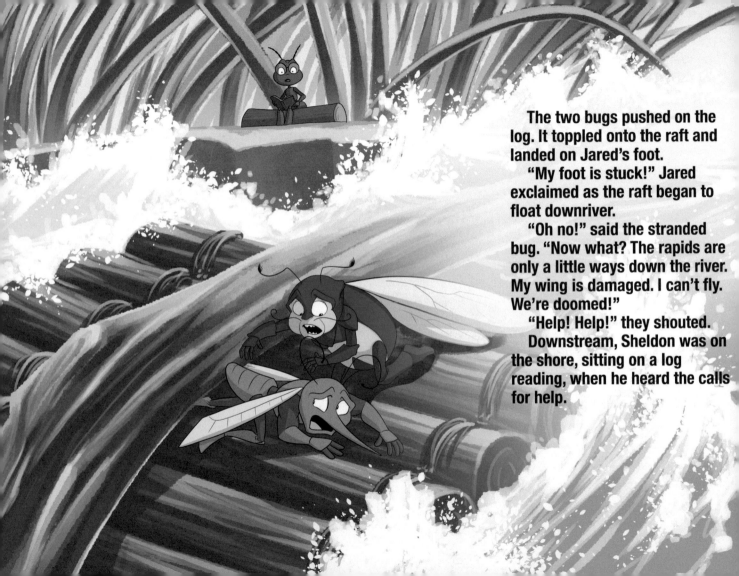

The two bugs pushed on the log. It toppled onto the raft and landed on Jared's foot.

"My foot is stuck!" Jared exclaimed as the raft began to float downriver.

"Oh no!" said the stranded bug. "Now what? The rapids are only a little ways down the river. My wing is damaged. I can't fly. We're doomed!"

"Help! Help!" they shouted.

Downstream, Sheldon was on the shore, sitting on a log reading, when he heard the calls for help.

Sheldon immediately went to work. He tore apart pieces of grass and quickly twisted them into a rope.

"Hold on, I'm coming!" he exclaimed.

"Please hurry!" called the stranded bug.

"You can do this, buddy! I know you can!" Jared yelled.

Sheldon hung from a tree branch over the river and lowered the grass rope over the raft.

Just as Jared and the stranded bug reached for the rope, Sheldon lost his footing and plunged into the water.

Sheldon splashed into the water, falling right next to the raft as they all drifted down toward the rapids.

"Grab my nose! I'll pull you in!" Jared yelled.

"No, you can't! What if I break it?" gasped Sheldon.

"Just grab it. I'll be fine," Jared replied.

Sheldon grabbed his nose and Jared yanked his head back and pulled him up onto the raft.

Together the three bugs lifted
the log and freed Jared.
Downstream, the rocks and
rapids drew closer and closer.

"We need to get off this raft before it breaks up on those rocks," Sheldon said.

"Oh my! How will we do that?" asked the stranded bug.

"Are you able to fly?" Sheldon asked Jared.

"Yeah, but the log damaged my wing," Jared answered. "I can barely get myself in the air, so I don't think I can lift you too. You are going to have to carry him."

"Um…OK. You get in the air," Sheldon told his friend. Then, addressing the stranded bug, said, "Sir, I am going to need you to jump on my back and hold on tight!"

"Oh my," the trembling stranded bug responded.

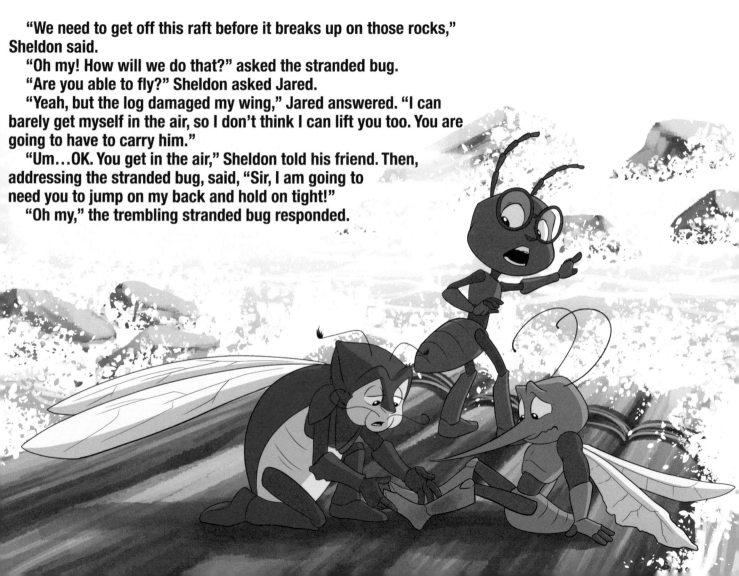

Jared flew, barely, above the raft.
Sheldon loaded the stranded bug on his back and jumped from the raft to the rocks and onto the shore.
Finally, they were safe!

Meanwhile, the race was over and the Beetle Brothers were celebrating their victory. Jared, Sheldon and the stranded bug were drying off while they stood in the audience.

With microphone in hand, the announcer addressed the Bug City residents:

"I will now introduce the bug of the hour, the most famous Protector Bug of all time, the bug responsible for choosing our winners today. Colonel Simmons, will you please join me on the stage?"

Suddenly, the stranded bug's giant wings spread out and he lifted Jared and Sheldon up in the air, flying them high above the crowd.
"Colonel, I assume you have made your choice," the announcer smiled.

Colonel Simmons looked around.
"Get these Beetles off this stage and out of my sight," he said. "Sheldon and Jared, you are perfect examples of what it takes to be a Protector Bug. Jared, you stopped to save someone you didn't even know, even though it was going to cost you your dream. Sheldon, you put aside your fears to save a friend and an old bug who you had never met."

"Congratulations, you are both officially Protector Bugs!"

The Beetle Brothers had sulked away and the crowd went wild.

"Colonel, who is your third choice?" asked the announcer.

"Well, that's simple," the Colonel announced. "Sheldon, where is your father, Leonard? Years ago he gave up his spot as a Protector Bug in order to keep the city safe and raise you. He has done an amazing job and deserves his shot at the big game. Leonard, please come up on stage. You are never too old to be what you were meant to be."

"We did it, buddy! We're Protector Bugs!" Jared exclaimed.

"I can't believe it. It's like a dream! Dad, what do you think?" Sheldon asked.

"I think your mom was right all along," Leonard said. "I just didn't know she was talking to both of us."

"Right!" Sheldon's dad said. "You can be whatever you want, if you're willing to dream big and work hard for it. This is going to be awesome!"

Little did they know, the real work was just about to begin.

Made in the USA
Columbia, SC
09 September 2024

41329513R00022